E
JEN

D1377309

Possum in the House

Written by Kiersten Jensen
Illustrated by Tony Oliver

Gareth Stevens Children's Books
Milwaukee

2

There's a possum in the house
and he's hiding in the pantry.
"Help, help!" screamed Dad.
"Oh drat!" yelled Mom.
CRUNCH, CRUNCH went the cornflakes.
"Screech, screech!" went the possum
as he ran into the . . .

3

. . . KITCHEN!

4

5

6

There's a possum in the kitchen
and he's hiding in the cupboard.
"Help, help!" screamed Mom.
"Oh drat!" yelled Dad.
CLATTER, CLATTER went the pots.
"Screech, screech!" went the possum
as he ran into the . . .

7

. . . LAUNDRY!

8

The WARNING text on the washing machine reads:

WARNING
Do not put your hand
in spin basket...

9

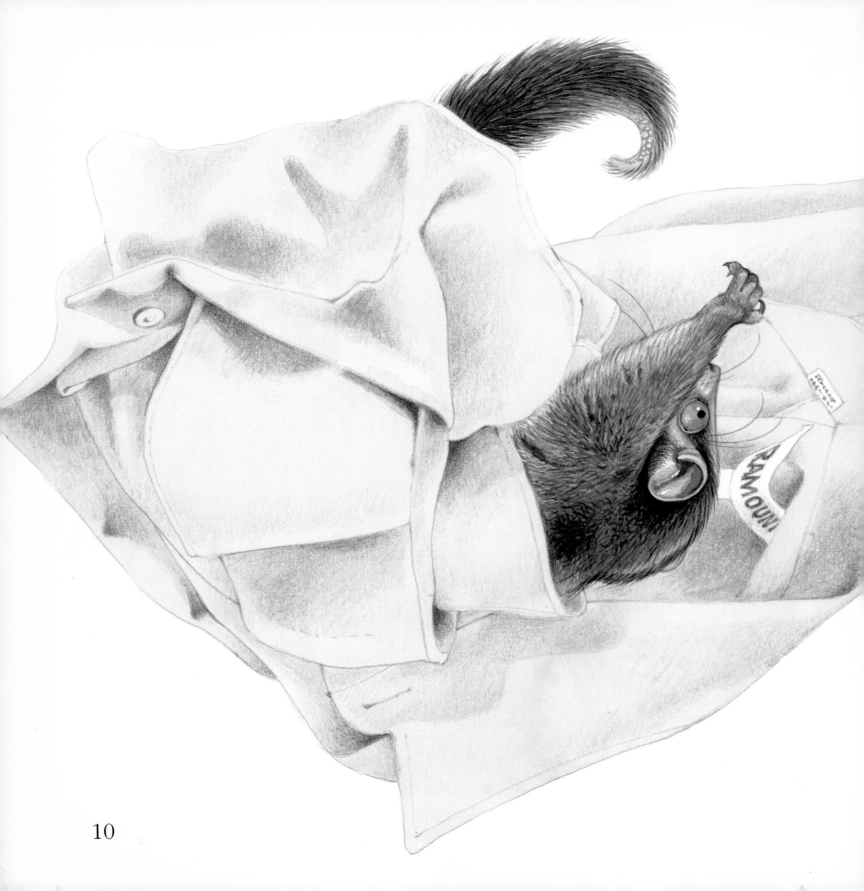

10

There's a possum in the laundry
and he's hiding in the basket.
"Help, help!" screamed Dad.
"Oh drat!" yelled Mom.
RIP, RIP went the shirts.
"Screech, screech!" went the possum
as he ran into the . . .

. . . STUDY!

12

14

There's a possum in the study
and he's hiding in the bookshelves.
"Help, help!" screamed Mom.
"Oh drat!" yelled Dad.
RUSTLE, RUSTLE went the pages.
"Screech, screech!" went the possum
as he ran into the . . .

CAMILLA FOX
ON SILVER WINS
BEST OF SHOW

KATE SIMONSEN
VOTED MOST
BEAUTIFUL BABY

. . . DEN!

16

There's a possum in the den
and he's hiding by the stereo.
"Help, help!" screamed Dad.
"Oh drat!" yelled Mom.
SCRATCH, SCRATCH went the records.
"Screech, screech!" went the possum
as he ran into the . . .

. . . BATHROOM!

There's a possum in the bathroom
and he's hiding in the drawer.
"Help, help!" screamed Mom.
"Oh drat!" yelled Dad.
SQUIRT, SQUIRT went the toothpaste.
"Screech, screech!" went the possum
as he jumped into the . . .

23

. . . TOILET!

24

26

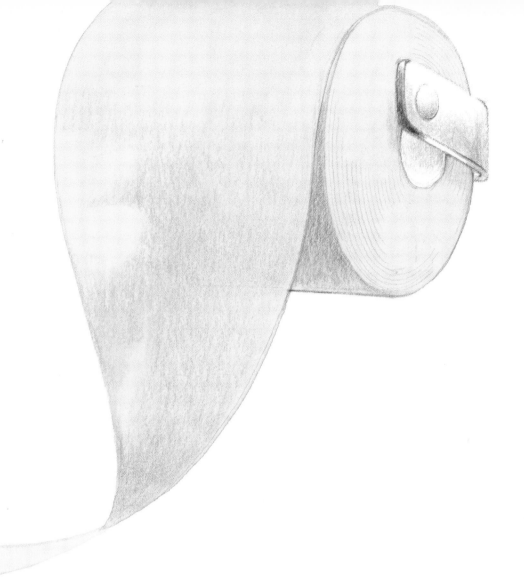

There's a possum in the bathroom
and he's hiding in the toilet!
"Help, help!" screamed Dad.
"Oh drat!" yelled Mom.
SPLASH, SPLASH went the water.
"Screech, screech!" went the possum
as he ran into . . .

. . . MY BEDROOM!

29

There's a possum in my bedroom
and he's sleeping on my bed!
"Poor thing," said Mom.
"He's tired," said Dad.
SNORE, SNORE went the possum.

SO WE LEFT HIM THERE!

31

Library of Congress Cataloging-in-Publication Data

Jensen, Kiersten, 1960-
       Possum in the house

       Summary: A frisky possum leads the family in a
       frenetic chase through the pantry, kitchen, bathroom,
       study, and other rooms of the house.
       [1. Opossums—fiction. 2. Dwellings—Fiction] I. Title.
       PZ7.J4343Po   1988   [E]   88-42910
       ISBN 1-55532-933-0

North American edition first published in 1989 by

Gareth Stevens Children's Books
7317 West Green Tree Road
Milwaukee, Wisconsin 53223, USA

1 2 3 4 5 6 7 8 9 94 93 92 91 90 89